Lucas

Evan

Matthew

Copyright © 2013 by NordSüd Verlag AG, CH-8005 Zürich, Switzerland.
First published in Switzerland under the title *Heute heiße ich Jakob!*
English text copyright © 2013 by NorthSouth Books Inc., New York 10016.
Translated by Nicholas Miller.

First published in the United States, Great Britain, Canada, Australia, and New Zealand in 2013 by NorthSouth Books Inc., an imprint of NordSüd Verlag AG, CH-8005 Zürich, Switzerland.
Distributed in the United States by NorthSouth Books Inc., New York 10016.

Library of Congress Cataloging-in-Publication Data is available.
ISBN: 978-0-7358-4134-5
Printed in Germany by Graisches Centrum Cuno GmbH & Co., KG, 39240 Calbe, September 2013.
1 3 5 7 9 • 10 8 6 4 2
www.northsouth.com

FSC
www.fsc.org
MIX
Paper from
responsible sources
FSC® C043106

Marie Hübner · Iris Wolfermann

Call Me Jacob!

North
South

Matthew stood in front of the mirror.

Suddenly, he said, "Mom, I don't like my name. I want to be called Jacob."

"Jacob?" asked his mother. "Like your cousin, who skateboards so well? That's a lovely name, but I'm not sure you need to be called the same thing."

Matthew—now Jacob—put on his pajamas.

"I just think the name is cool!"

Matthew's mother chuckled and said, "So, does that mean from now on I should call you Jacob?"

"Exactly!"

"Then, sleep well, Jacob."

Matthew couldn't wait to share his new name with his friend Max.
Mrs. Winkle, the baker's wife, waved to him. "Good morning, Matthew!"
"My name isn't Matthew anymore. From now on, my name is Jacob!"
"I had no idea," said Mrs. Winkle. "Well, then have yourself a wonderful
day, Jacob."

"Hey, Max, I have a new name!" Matthew yelled. "From now on, you can call me Jacob!"

"Jacob? Why 'Jacob'? That's silly."

"I thought it was a nice name," Matthew said.

"It's all right," Max said. "Jacob it is then. I just have to get used to it."

LUCAS

Volleyball was next. Matthew, now Jacob, was sure he'd be picked last. And, of course, Lucas would be picked first. Lucas was as fast as lightning and never missed the ball.

If only I would be picked first, thought Matthew.

Later that evening Matthew's mother came into his room.

"Good night, Jacob," she said.

"Mom, I've thought about it, and Jacob isn't as cool of a name as I'd wanted," said Matthew. "I want my name to be Lucas."

"Lucas?" asked Matthew's mother. "Isn't Lucas your classmate who is so good at volleyball?"

Matthew looked away from her. "Yeah, so? I didn't even think of that. I just think it's a good name, that's all."

"Ah!" His mother nodded. "Then, good night—Lucas."

The next morning the newspaper seller shouted, "Hi, Matthew!"

"My name isn't Matthew. My name is Lucas!" said Matthew, now Lucas. Today he felt big and strong.

"Well, Lucas! All clear then!" said the newspaper seller with a wave good-bye.

    In school, even before Max could say hello, Matthew yelled,
"By the way, now my name is Lucas."

    "Lucas? Like the volleyball showoff in our class?" asked Max.

    "It doesn't have anything to do with him. It's just a good name,"
said Matthew.

    "C'mon! They're announcing the winners of the math competition.
You definitely have a good chance of winning." He poked his friend
in his side. "Lucas!"

Matthew—not Jacob, but Lucas now—felt very excited. He hoped that he would win a prize. In math, he was the best—or at least the best in his class.

They read off the names for first, second, and third place. But they didn't say "Matthew," and they didn't say "Lucas." Instead, first place went to Evan, a fourth grader. Just like last year.

Matthew came in seventh place and got a certificate.
Max patted him on the shoulder and said, "Cool! A
certificate! That's really cool."

"Mom, I think I want to change my name again," Matthew said to his mother. "I want to be called Evan. Now, that is a good name."

"Didn't you tell me that Evan Berger won a math prize today?" asked his mother. "Don't feel sad about the contest. You did a good job. . . ."

"I AM NOT SAD. THE NAME IS JUST MUCH COOLER!" Matthew said, giving his mother a determined look.

"I'm sorry. I just thought—well, sleep tight, Evan," his mother said, kissing him on the forehead.

The next day it was raining.
"Today you'll have to take the school bus," said his mother. "Otherwise, you'll get soaking wet."

When Matthew got on the bus, the driver said, "Good morning, Matthew. Lovely having you ride with us today."

"My name is Evan now," Matthew explained to him.

"Oh. Well, hopefully I can remember that—Evan," the bus driver said.

When Matthew saw Max he said, "By the way, my name isn't Lucas anymore. Now my name is Evan."

"Jeez, would you stick with one name? It's annoying," Max said. "Will you at least come with me to the library?"

"Of course," said Matthew. "But only if you call me Evan!"

"Sure thing, Evan!" Max said as they ran to the library.

Later that day, Matthew's father said, "Anna came by and dropped off a letter for you, Matthew."

"He's called Evan now," his mother said, smiling.

"Well, if that's the case, then this letter isn't for you after all," his father said. "It says 'For Matthew.'"

Matthew's—not Jacob's, not Lucas's—now Evan's face turned bright red. He was so excited about Anna's letter.

"Dad, can I please have the letter? You know that it is really for me!"

His father grinned and handed him the letter.

Matthew beamed as he read the letter. Anna sent him—Matthew—an invitation. Unbelievable! He tucked it gently under his pillow.

Dear Matthew!
Next week is my birthday, and I want to take a bike ride out to our cabin in the woods. I would love it if you could come with us. We're meeting at 2 p.m. on Saturday at our house.

Sincerely yours,

Anna

The next morning Matthew was in a great mood. He whistled to himself.

"Good morning, Jacob!" Mrs. Winkle, the baker's wife, shouted.

Matthew waved and crossed the street.

"That's our Lucas!" said the newspaper seller.

Matthew smiled back.

The bus driver leaned out the window and yelled, "Hey, Evan, need a ride today?"

Matthew waved and kept walking.

"So, what's your name today?" Max asked his friend.

"Matthew!" said Matthew with a smile. "What else would it be?"

Max raised his eyebrows. "Oh, you mean like the *old* Matthew?"

Matthew started to laugh and said, "Or like the new one!"

Jacob

Matthew